The PURPLE Paper

Asa Jwa

Archway Publishing books may be ordered through booksellers or by contacting:

Archway Publishing
1663 Liberty Drive
Bloomington, IN 47403
www.archwaypublishing.com
844-669-3957

ISBN: 978-1-6657-5109-4 (sc)
ISBN: 978-1-6657-5108-7 (hc)
ISBN: 978-1-6657-5107-0 (e)

Library of Congress Control Number: 2023919203

Print information available on the last page.

Archway Publishing rev. date: 1/11/2024

The **PURPLE** Paper

Once upon a time, there was a little girl named Asianni. She and her grandmother, Mom Mom, were walking one rainy day. They saw a purple paper.

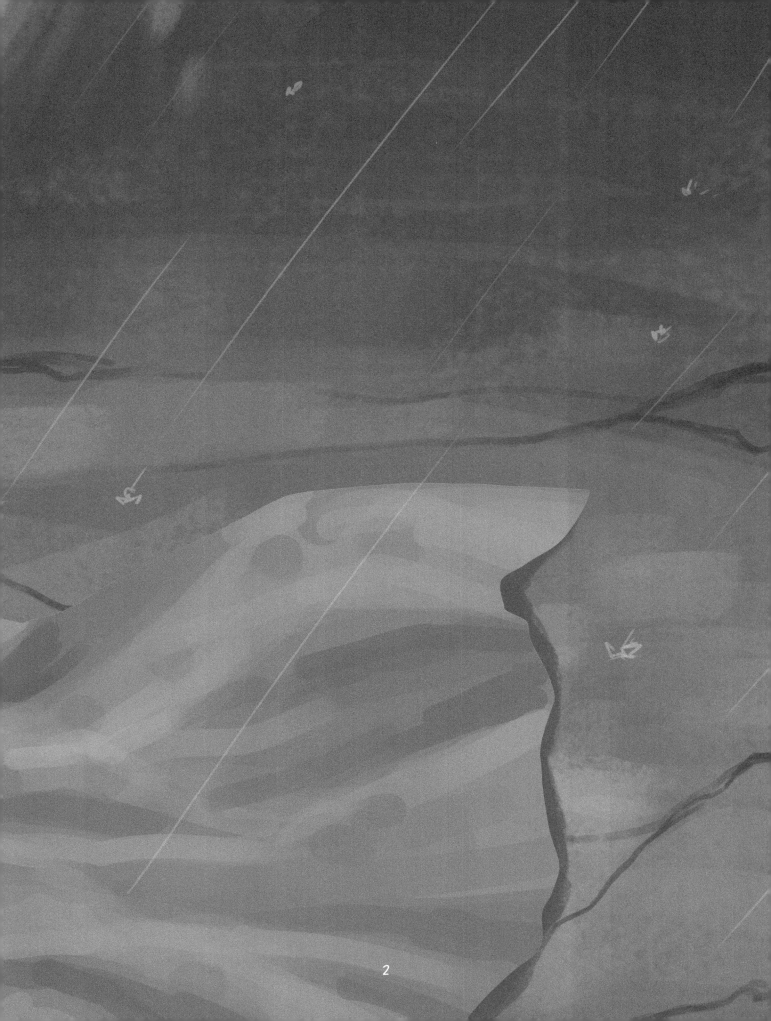

The paper made them wonder, where had it come from? How was it abandoned to the sidewalk half in a water puddle? The paper seemed to tell the story of its birth and travels.

4

The paper started as a tree. Let's call our tree purple tree. Our purple tree was a home to birds, ladybugs, and squirrels.

The mayor in the town where
purple tree grew sent for
our tree to be cut down.

From there, purple tree went by truck to be changed into paper.

From paper, a special small part of purple tree was taken to a section of the factory, which had lots of beautiful dye colors.

The special section of paper was dipped in purple dye and set to dry. After drying, purple paper tree received a new name—purple paper. Purple paper now had a new life and purpose. Purple paper now had a very important job.

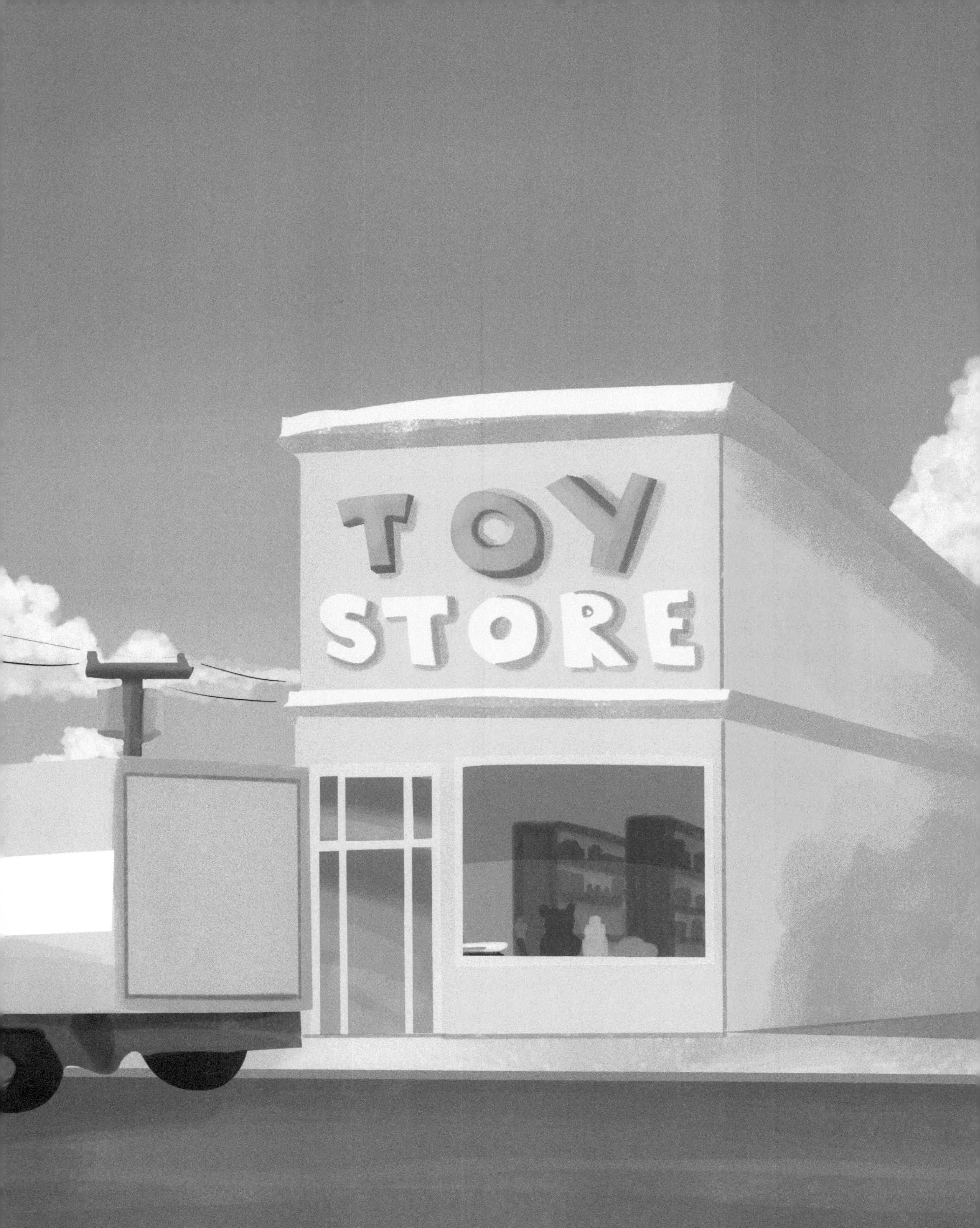
TOY
STORE

The job was to wrap a present. Not just any present. Purple paper was born to wrap a toy truck for a little boy. The little boy was so excited looking at the purple paper wrapped gift.

He was very happy with his new toy truck. He intended to bring his gift and the special paper home. But in his excitement, he accidentally dropped a piece of the precious purple paper.

The purple paper was once a grand tall tree, which was once home to birds, squirrels, and ladybugs.

This piece of purple paper
had one more job.

This piece of purple paper needed to be dropped and forgotten, only to be spotted by Asianni and Mom Mom. This piece of purple paper was born to inspire this story.

Thank you, purple paper. Thank you, birds, squirrels, and ladybugs. Thank you, town mayor and paper factory. Thank you to all the beautiful colored dyes. Thank you, little boy with the new toy truck. Thank you purple paper.

Lastly, yet just as important, thank you dear reader for letting Asianni and I share the joy and journey of our crumpled but beautiful purple paper.

The End

Milton Keynes UK
Ingram Content Group UK Ltd.
UKHW050227080224
437310UK00003B/124